THE ABOMINABLE SNOWMAN MYSTERY

By Shannon Penney ▪ Illustrated by Duendes del Sur
Hello Reader — Level 1

SCHOLASTIC INC.

New York Toronto London Auckland Sydney
Mexico City New Delhi Hong Kong Buenos Aires

ISBN 0-439-78549-9

12 11 10 9 8 7 6 5   7 8 9 10/0

Printed in the U.S.A.
First printing, November 2005

and his friends were on vacation in the . They were staying in a .

, , and the rest of the gang were ready to ski and have fun in the .

There were lots of fun activities!

Everyone bundled up. They each wore a 🧢, 🧣, 🧥, 👢, and 🧤.

👧 and 👩 made pretty ❄s.

The gang even had a ⛄ fight!

[Scooby] was having a lot of fun, until he saw something off in the distance. It looked like a giant [wave] monster! He tugged on [Shaggy]'s sleeve.

"Zoinks!" cried [Shaggy]. "It's the [monster]! Let's get out of here, [Scooby]!"

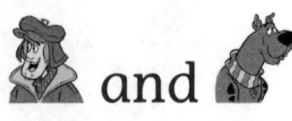 and  ran into the . Their

friends didn't know they were

running from the .

"Good idea! Let's all go inside to

warm up," said.

Everyone left their outside the

back of the .

"Once we're warm and dry again,

we can go skiing!" said .

Inside the 🏠 , the gang sat on the 🛋️ . They drank hot chocolate and 🍬 from big ☕ .

🐕 and 👤 played games in front of the 🔥 . They had so much fun, they forgot about the ⛄ .

After a while, everyone was toasty and ready to ski!

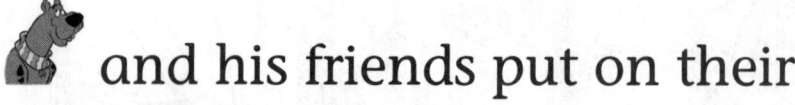 and his friends put on their

 s, s, s, , and again. They went out the side

and down the .

But something was missing.

Their 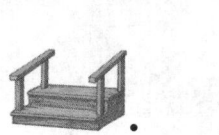 had disappeared!

"Oh, no!" said 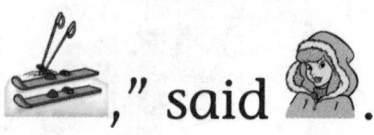.

"We can't go skiing without our 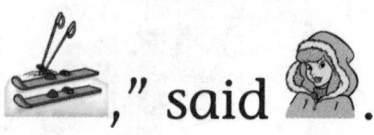," said 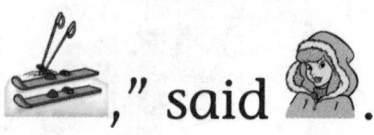.

"Zoinks!" cried 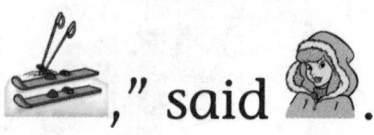, pointing into the distance. "It's the 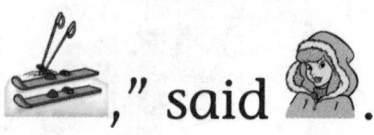! I'll bet he took our 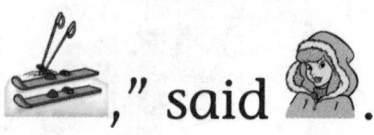, and now he's after us!"

"Let's look around,"  said.

"Maybe someone just moved our

."

 walked through the deep

around the . He didn't see the

 anywhere.

When  came back,  and

were huddled together, shivering.

But they were not cold. They were

afraid of the !

"Maybe someone moved our 🎿 inside," 👧 said. She and 👧 walked up the 🪜 and through the 🚪. But the 🎿 were not inside.

When the girls came back out, 🐕 and 👧 had a 🧣 tied over their eyes. That way, they couldn't see the 👹!

"The 🧟 took our ⛷️!" 👧 cried,

pointing into the distance.

"That's just a big ❄️drift," said

🧥. "The 🧟 would have left big

👣 in the ❄️. And there were no

👣 at all when we came outside."

"You're right!" 👩 said. "And I

think I know where our ⛷️ are."

dug down in the [snow] and pulled up a pair of [skis].

"It must have snowed while we were inside," she said. "The [snow] covered up our [skis], and our [footprint]s from before!"

[Scooby] pulled his [skis] from under the [snow]. The [monster] didn't take them after all!

"Rooby-dooby-do!" [Scooby] cheered.

Did you spot all the picture clues in this Scooby-Doo mystery?

Each picture clue is on a flash card. Ask a grown-up to cut out the flash cards. Then try reading the words on the back of the cards. The pictures will be your clue.

Reading is fun with Scooby-Doo!